THE JUNGLE BOOK

Adapted from the Mowgli stories

by Rudyard Kipling

A GOLDEN BOOK • NEW YORK

Western Publishing Company, Inc., Racine, Wisconsin

© 1967 The Walt Disney Company. All rights reserved. Printed in the U.S.A. by Western Publishing Company, Inc.
No part of this book may be reproduced or copied in any form without written permission from the copyright owner.
GOLDEN®, GOLDEN & DESIGN®, A GOLDEN BOOK®, and A LITTLE GOLDEN BOOK® are trademarks
of Western Publishing Company, Inc. Library of Congress Catalog Card Number: 83-83362 ISBN 0-307-00326-4/
ISBN 0-307-60245-1 (lib. bdg.)   G H I J

Many strange legends are told of the jungles of far-off India. They speak of Bagheera the black panther, of Baloo the bear. They tell of Kaa the sly python, and of the Lord of the Jungle, the great tiger, Shere Khan. But of all the legends, none is so strange as the story of a small boy named Mowgli.

The story began when a child, left all alone in the jungle, was found by Bagheera the panther. He could not give the small, helpless "man-cub" care and nourishment, so Bagheera took him to the den of a wolf family with young cubs of their own.

That is how it happened that Mowgli, as the man-cub came to be called, was raised among the wolves. All the jungle folk were his friends.

Bagheera took Mowgli on long walks and taught him jungle lore.

Baloo, the bumbling bear, played games with
Mowgli and taught him to live a life of ease. There
were coconuts for the cracking, bananas for the
peeling, sweet and juicy pawpaws to pick from
jungle trees.

Hathi, the proud old leader of the
elephant herd, tried to train young
Mowgli in military drill as he led his
troop trumpeting down the
jungle trails.

Sly old Kaa the python would have loved to squeeze Mowgli tight in his coils. Mowgli's friends warned him against Kaa.

It was Shere Khan the tiger who was the real danger to Mowgli. That was because Shere Khan, like all tigers, had a hatred of man.

Ten times the season of rains had come to the jungle while Mowgli made his home with the wolf family. Then Shere Khan returned to the wolves' hunting grounds.

The wolf pack met at Council Rock when next the moon was full. "As you know," said Akela, the leader of the pack, "Shere Khan the tiger has returned. If he learns that our pack is harboring a man-cub, danger will be doubled for all our families. Are we agreed that the man-cub must go?"

Out of the shadows stepped Bagheera the panther. "I brought the man-cub to the pack," he said. "It is my duty to see him safely out of the jungle. I know a man-village not far away where he will be well cared for."

So it was arranged, and when the greenish light of the jungle morning slipped through the leaves, Bagheera and Mowgli set out.

All day they walked, and when night fell they slept on a high branch of a giant banyan tree. All this seemed like an adventure to Mowgli. But when he learned that he was to leave the jungle, he was horrified.

"No!" cried Mowgli. "The jungle is my home. I can take care of myself. I will stay!"

He slipped down a length of trailing vine and rudely ran away.

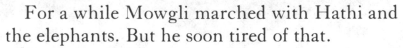

For a while Mowgli marched with Hathi and the elephants. But he soon tired of that.

Then he found Baloo bathing in a jungle pool. Mowgli joined him for a dip.

Suddenly down swooped the monkey folk, the noisy, foolish *Bandar-log*. They had snatched Mowgli from the pool before Baloo knew what was happening.

They tossed him through the air from hand to hand, and swung him away through the trees.

Off in the jungle, Bagheera heard Mowgli's cry and came with a leap and a bound.

"The monkeys have stolen Mowgli away!" gasped Baloo.

Off raced Bagheera and Baloo to the ruined city where the monkeys made their home.

They found Mowgli a prisoner of the monkey king.

"Teach me the secret of fire," the monkey king ordered Mowgli. "The magic of fire will frighten even Shere Khan. With it I shall be the equal of men. Until I know the secret, you are my prisoner."

It took quite a fight for Bagheera and Baloo to rescue Mowgli that time!

"Now you see," they told him, "why you must go to the man-village to be safe."

But alas, that foolish boy would not understand. He kicked up his heels and ran away again.

This time his wanderings led him to where Shere Khan lay waiting in the high grass, smiling a hungry smile.

When Mowgli caught sight of the tiger, Shere Khan asked, "Well, man-cub, aren't you going to run?"

But Mowgli did not have the wisdom to be afraid. "Why should I run?" he asked, staring Shere Khan in the eye as the tiger gathered himself for a spring. "I'm not afraid of you."

"That foolish boy!" growled Bagheera, who had
crept close just in time to hear Mowgli.

Both Bagheera and Baloo flung themselves upon
the Lord of the Jungle, to save Mowgli once more.

They were brave and strong, but the tiger was mighty of tooth and claw.

There was a flash of lightning, and a dead tree nearby caught fire. Mowgli snatched a burning branch and waved it in Shere Khan's face. The tiger, terrified, ran away. Mowgli was very pleased with himself as he strutted between the two weary warriors, Bagheera and Baloo.

Suddenly Mowgli stopped. From ahead came a sound that was strange to him. He peeked through the brush. It was the song of a village girl who had come to fill her water jar.

As he listened to the soft
notes of her song, Mowgli felt
strange inside. He felt that he
must follow her. Mowgli crept
up the path to the village,
following the girl and her song.

Baloo and Bagheera watched the small figure
as long as it could be seen. When Mowgli
vanished inside the village gate, Bagheera
sighed a deep sigh.

"It is just as it should be, Baloo," he said.
"Our Mowgli is safe in the man-village at last.
He has found his true home."